Fairy Unicorns

Magic Forest

Zanna Davidson

Illustrated by Nuno Alexandre Vieira

Meet the Unicorns

Zoe

Astra

Sorrel

Unicorn King

Nimbus

Orion

Lily

Shadow

Towering Cliffs

Jewelled Tree

Cloud Castle

Unicorn King's Castle

Lyra Tree

Ragged Cliffs

Sparkling Lake

EASTERN SEA

Unicorn Valley

N
W E
S

Contents

Chapter One

It was the beginning of the summer holidays and Zoe and her cousin Holly were staying with their Great-Aunt May. Zoe visited her great-aunt every year but, for the first time, she couldn't help feeling something strange was going on.

Every night, just as she was going to sleep, she'd heard the creak of Holly's bedroom door, followed by a faint whisper of footsteps. Her cousin was definitely up to something! Tonight was Holly's last night staying with their aunt, and Zoe was determined to find out what was happening.

She peered out of her bedroom window, into the moonlit garden below. Her plan was to watch and wait. At last, she saw a shadowy figure slip down the path. It was her cousin, outside in the garden! Zoe watched her for a moment and then, as quietly as she could, she crept out of her bedroom and began to tiptoe down the stairs.

She couldn't help thinking it might have something to do with the picture of fairy ponies that hung on the wall in Holly's attic bedroom. It showed magical ponies streaming out from an oak tree, each one a different colour, with gossamer-light, shimmering wings. Every now and then, Zoe would catch Holly gazing at the picture with a strange expression on her face. It wasn't the look you had when you liked something, it was more a kind of...*wonder*. A few times, Zoe had asked about the picture, but Holly had only shaken her head and changed the subject.

Zoe opened the back door into the garden and stepped outside into the silvery moonlight. The grass was wet and springy beneath her bare feet and the soft night wind brushed against her cheek. She could see Holly, a little way ahead of her, standing beneath the huge oak tree at the end of the garden. Carefully, Zoe made her way towards her cousin.

As she approached, she could hear Holly chanting something beneath her breath. It sounded like a spell, but Zoe couldn't quite catch the words. Then Holly reached for a tiny, sparkling bag that hung around her

neck. Zoe's heart began to beat faster.

What is it? she wondered. The bag looked magical, glowing in the moonlight. Holly dipped her fingers inside, and began to sprinkle herself with a shimmering, golden dust. Zoe looked on in amazement, as some of the dust caught on the breeze and wafted over to her.

For a moment, the golden dust hung in the air. Zoe stretched out her arms so that it settled, light as thistledown, on her fingertips. She looked over at Holly to see what she'd do next, but...her cousin had vanished.

"Holly?" Zoe called out.

There was no answer. Then something stranger still began to happen...everything around her started to grow. The oak tree, always big, now loomed above her, as if it belonged in the land of giants. Next, even the grasses were towering over her. Great-Aunt May's garden had become a jungle, with rocks the size of cliffs and flowers as big as the sun.

What's going on? Zoe wondered. Then she realized...it wasn't that everything was growing. *She* was shrinking. And so had Holly.

Zoe could see Holly, running into a gap between the roots of the oak tree. *It must have been a magic dust,* thought Zoe. *Is Holly magic?*

With a hundred questions whirling through her mind, Zoe called out for Holly to stop, but she was already too far ahead to hear.

I'll have to go after her, thought Zoe. *I have to*

find out what's going on.

For a moment she hesitated, nervous about what might lie ahead, but another part of her was longing to explore. "Oh well," she said to her fairy-sized self, "there's nothing else for it now." Her heart pounding with excitement, Zoe stepped between the roots, and saw a tunnel stretch out before her. She took a deep breath and ran after her cousin.

At first, the way was lit by a glimmering light. The oak walls were golden brown, and the ground was soft and warm beneath her feet. It felt like sand on a beach.

I really am inside the oak tree, thought Zoe. *Something extraordinary is happening.*

"I'm on a magical journey…" she whispered to herself. "Where will it end?"

Breathless from running, Zoe rounded the corner…and was plunged into sudden darkness. She couldn't even see her hands when she waved them in front of her face.

"Holly!" she called out. "Holly?"

She was met only with silence. It was as if her cousin had disappeared, taking the light with her.

Zoe reached out, feeling reassured as her fingertips touched the warm oak walls. Curiously, she didn't feel afraid. The oak tree had a kind of magic to it, somehow letting her know she was safe here.

Using her hands to guide her, Zoe stumbled on until, at last, she saw light. It was then she noticed that there were other pathways, breaking away from the main one, heading off in a myriad of different directions.

"Which path has Holly taken?" Zoe wondered. There was only one way to find out. Zoe began to run again and, as she drew nearer the end of the tunnel, she could just make out a blue sky and a glade of silvery trees.

"Wow!" Zoe whispered in wonder. "I've found a magical world..."

Before her, wandering through the silvery glade, were beautiful winged creatures. Zoe blinked and looked again, almost expecting the vision to fade. But they were still there — the most dazzling creatures she had ever seen.

Some were pure white, others were glimmering green and azure blue…all the colours of the rainbow. Each had a spiralling pearly horn and beautiful, butterfly wings. Zoe held her breath, worried if she did anything they might vanish before her eyes.

"They're almost like the fairy ponies in the picture," Zoe realized. "But these are… fairy unicorns!"

Chapter Two

For a moment, Zoe just watched the
unicorns in wonder. None of them
seemed to have noticed her and she
gazed and gazed, unable to believe
how beautiful they were. Their
coats gleamed in the sunlight, their
hoofs sparkled and their wings were
as delicate as gossamer.

At last, she tore her gaze away from the unicorns and began to look at the world around her. The grass was so bright and lush it was as if it had been sprinkled with emeralds. The silver bark of the trees glittered and shone. Above her head, the leaves were awash with colour – rustling pink, yellow, blue, green and gold in the breeze.

Then she heard a voice behind her. Zoe turned around to see a little white face peering through the branches of a nearby tree. It was a unicorn. Her horn shone like an ocean pearl and she had large dark eyes, which gazed at Zoe shyly. The unicorn trotted out from between the trees until she was standing just a little way from Zoe, as if scared to come any nearer.

"Don't be afraid," said Zoe. "I'm not going to hurt you."

The little unicorn came closer, nervously pawing the ground with one of her sparkling hoofs.

"Who are you?" she asked.

Her voice was musical, both lilting and soothing, in a way that made Zoe think of water tumbling over stones. She noticed, too, that the unicorn's coat was patterned with silvery stars.

"My name is Zoe," she began.

"Are you a…human?" asked the unicorn.

"Yes," said Zoe, laughing.

At the sound, the unicorn took a step backwards in surprise.

"Sorry," said Zoe. "I didn't mean to startle you. It's just no one's ever asked me that before."

"I've *heard* of humans," said the unicorn, stepping closer, "but I've never seen one."

She began inspecting Zoe with curious eyes, as if unable to believe she had two legs instead of four.

"How did you come to be here?" she asked at last.

"I don't really know," Zoe confessed. "I was following my cousin, Holly, and something *magical* happened. I shrank down to fairy size and found a tunnel between the roots of an oak tree. I lost Holly along the way, but then I saw a light and I followed it…and came out here!"

The unicorn continued to watch her intently.

"I know it sounds strange, but it's true," said Zoe. "I didn't even know unicorns existed until now. I thought they were only in stories."

"We're real," said the unicorn, "but we keep ourselves hidden from the human world. I have never met your cousin, but we have heard of a human visitor to Pony Island, not far from here, where the Fairy Ponies live. As for the oak tree — we call it the Great Oak. It connects our world to yours."

"So it *is* a magical tree…" said Zoe. "And what's your name? I mean, do unicorns have names?"

"Of course we have names," laughed the unicorn. "Mine's Astra."

"Astra," Zoe repeated. "It suits you."

And it did. The name sounded beautiful and ethereal, just like the little unicorn.

"It means star," Astra explained.

"Oh!" said Zoe. "Just like the silvery marks on your coat."

But at this, Astra hung her head.

"I'm the only unicorn that has them," she whispered. "All the others have beautiful pure coats. Only mine has these…speckles."

"They're not speckles!" said Zoe. "They look like star dust. But I'm just the same."

She held out her arms. "Look at me," she said. "I'm covered in freckles."

"Oh!" said Astra, smiling, and as their eyes met, Zoe felt a connection with the shy little unicorn, as if this could be the beginning of a magical friendship. But then Astra's gaze rested on something behind Zoe and her smile faded.

"You are very welcome here," Astra went on, her voice mournful now, "but you've come at a terrible time."

Zoe turned and followed Astra's gaze, beyond the glade and into the forest. She noticed for the first time that not all the trees had the same shining bark and glittering rainbow leaves. Some were blackened, with drooping branches and fallen leaves. A few had turned limp and appeared bowed down beneath the weight of their branches.

"What's happening?" asked Zoe.

Astra shook her head. "We're not really sure," she whispered. "It started this morning.

We've never seen anything like it before. It's the trees – their trunks have always shone silver, day and night, and their leaves have always lit up the sky with their colours. But today…"

She stopped for a moment, as if too upset to go on.

"What?" questioned Zoe, unable to help herself. "What is it?"

"It's happening all over the island," Astra went on. "The trees…they're dying."

Chapter Three

Zoe looked again at the dying trees, at their
warped and twisted trunks and leafless
branches. She saw some other unicorns
standing in a circle, talking together in
urgent voices, their brows furrowed.

"Isn't it terrible?" said Astra. "There
seems to be a pattern. First the leaves fall,
then the branches droop and then finally…

the tree just crumples."

"Is there nothing you can do to save them?" asked Zoe.

"Nothing that we know of," said a voice behind her.

Zoe turned to find another unicorn watching them. This one was much larger than Astra, and seemed older. There was wisdom in her black eyes. Her coat had a beautiful forest-like glow and on her head she wore a circlet of willow, woven round with ivy.

"This is my mother, Sorrel," said Astra. "She is Guardian of the Trees. Mother, this is Zoe."

"Welcome," said Sorrel. "A human visitor to Unicorn Island is something very special. I can only hope that you have been sent to help us.

As Astra said, we've tried everything we can to save the trees, but none of our medicines have worked, and neither have our spells or enchantments. If the trees carry on dying like this, soon there will be none left on the island."

"What will happen then?" asked Zoe, fearfully.

"The trees protect us from the elements," said
Sorrel. "They provide shelter, homes and food
for the unicorns and all the woodland animals.
Without them, the island as we know it will be
gone for ever."

Astra ran to her mother. "We can't let that
happen," she said. "What about the Unicorn
King? We have to tell him!"

Sorrel saw Zoe's questioning look.

"The Unicorn King is our ruler," she explained. "He lives on the other side of the island, in a castle carved from rock. He is a good king and has always helped us in times of trouble…"

"He'll help us now!" said Astra.

"I've tried calling him," said Sorrel, gently, "but he hasn't come. I've rung the wind chimes and sounded the horn…I don't understand it. I'd go to him myself, but I can't leave my trees, or the woodland animals. They need me here to comfort them."

"What about the other unicorns?" asked Zoe. "Can't one of them go?"

But in the glade beyond, Zoe could see that the other unicorns were now trying to support the weakened trees. As she watched, another tree began to wilt, its trunk buckling. One of the unicorns rushed over to it, desperately trying to keep the tree upright, while another unicorn cast spells from his horn.

"I know!" said Astra. "We could go!"

She looked at Zoe as she spoke, and Zoe nodded in agreement. She had only just arrived on the island, but already she couldn't bear to see it destroyed.

Sorrel looked worried. "But Astra, you've never travelled that far across the island on your own before."

"I know the way," said Astra, eagerly. "I head east until I reach the white cliff face, and then the Unicorn King's castle is at the top of the waterfall."

"And I'd be with her," added Zoe, excited at the thought of being able to help. "So she wouldn't be on her own."

Sorrel paused for a moment, deep in thought.

"We do need help," she said at last, "and the time for waiting is over. You may go, but take great care. Keep flying straight, Astra, that's the quickest way. Be careful not to go too close to the mountains. I heard there was some rock fall on the western hills…"

"We'll be fine," insisted Astra.

"*Fly…?*" interrupted Zoe. "I've never ridden a horse before, let alone flown on a unicorn…"

As if sensing her fear, Sorrel came towards her.

"Do not be afraid, Zoe. Astra will fly swift and sure," she said, smiling at her daughter.

"I have trained her well. She will keep you safe."

"How do I…?" Zoe began, but before she could say more, Astra was at her side, bending her forelegs so that her sloping back was waist-high with Zoe.

"Climb on her back, Zoe," Sorrel said gently. "I have seen pictures in storybooks of humans on the backs of unicorns. Your legs should be just behind Astra's wings."

"You've seen pictures in storybooks?" said Zoe. "So you're not actually sure if this works?"

Sorrel laughed. "Ah!" she said. "But all the best stories are true."

Zoe hesitated, but Astra gave her a shy smile, and once again Zoe felt the connection between them. Trustingly, she climbed on Astra's back and leaned forward, tangling her hands in Astra's mane. Her new friend's coat was silky soft and Zoe breathed in the comforting warm honey smell of her coat.

I can't believe I'm about to fly on the back of a unicorn, she thought.

"Fly well," said Sorrel, "and good luck."

Before Zoe could think any more about it, Astra was beating her gossamer-light wings and they were rising up, up into the air. Zoe gasped as the ground disappeared beneath her and held on even more tightly. For a moment,

she shut her
eyes, trying
to still the
giddy feeling
inside her. Then
the motion changed. They were
no longer rising upwards but flying fast and
free across the sky. The wind was rushing
through her hair so that it streamed out behind
her and she could feel the pounding of Astra's
wings as they soared through the airy blue.
Zoe forced her eyes open and gazed around.

"I'm not too heavy for you, am I?" she asked.

"Not at all," Astra replied. "I've flown with
baskets of berries and apples on my back
before and you're much lighter than that.
Look down now if you can. We're coming out

of the Silvery Glade. You can see the rest

of Unicorn Island."

Zoe steeled herself to look down...and

gasped. The view was so beautiful she forgot

her fear. Unfolding beneath her was a lush,

green valley, encircled by snow-capped

mountains. A river, sparkling like a sapphire,

wound its way across the valley floor. She could

just make out the dazzling coats of more unicorns, galloping along the riverbank. The next moment, they jumped into the river and disappeared from view.

"Those are the River Unicorns," said Astra. "They rarely leave the water. They must have heard what's been happening to the trees and come to see for themselves."

"Are there different kinds of unicorns, then?" asked Zoe, peering down to see if she could spot the River Unicorns again.

"Yes," Astra replied. "Each kind helps the King look after a different part of the island. The Flower Unicorns live in the meadows and care for the flowers and the bees and butterflies. The Snow Unicorns keep to the White Mountains and look after the animals of frost and snow. And then there are the Cloud Unicorns who live in a floating castle in the sky. They care for the clouds and the birds."

"Oh!" exclaimed Zoe. "I want to meet them *all*. What about your mum, Sorrel – she said she was Guardian of the Trees. What does she do?"

"The Guardians are the most magical of all

the unicorns, apart from the
King," said Astra. "They have
studied the spell books and
know the enchantments. My
mother is trying to train me up, so that one
day I'll be a Guardian of the Trees too…"

"Sorry," said Zoe. "Am I tiring you with all
my questions?"

"No, it's not that," Astra replied. "You'll
find out soon enough… You see, all unicorns
are born being able to do magic and some,
like my mother, are especially gifted." She
paused again. "Well, when I said *all*
unicorns," she added, her voice dropping to a
whisper, "I meant all unicorns except *me*. I'm
different, you see, just like the stars on my
coat. My mother says my magic will come

one day, when I least expect it, but I'm not sure I believe that any more."

From the catch in Astra's voice, Zoe could tell how much she minded. "I'm sorry," said Zoe. "But now I'm here, that makes two of us who can't do spells."

Astra smiled gratefully and Zoe hugged her more closely.

"We're nearly there now," said Astra, as if wanting to change the subject. "Can you see the castle? Look for where the water comes gushing out of the rocks."

"I can see the waterfall!" Zoe cried, as the water came into view, tumbling crystal clear down the smooth rocks. "But where's the castle?"

"Keep looking!" said Astra.

And then she saw it. The castle was carved
into the rock face
itself, white and gleaming
and almost hidden
from view. Its roof
was carpeted
with moss,
and ivy
trailed down
its sides,
so that
it seemed
a living
part of
the landscape.

Only when the breeze stirred did Zoe spot the flag, fluttering on the wind, bearing a silhouette of a black unicorn, bearing a crown.

"It's beautiful," Zoe breathed.

As they drew closer, she could hear the gushing torrent of the waterfall. Astra swept over its foaming spray and stretched out her wings to still her speed. Making a smooth arc through the sky, she came to land on a rocky ledge. From there, they climbed up twisting steps and trotted over a little bridge until they came to a pair of shining gates. Cautiously, Zoe slid from Astra's back, her legs feeling wobbly now that she was back on land.

A bell rope was hanging by the side of the gates. Astra took it in her teeth, pulling until the bell jangled, its sound echoing off the cliff faces all around. They waited a moment but there was no answer. Zoe shivered. She didn't know why but she suddenly felt nervous.

Astra caught her eye. "I feel it too," she said. "As if something's not quite right… Still, there's no turning back now."

Astra tapped one of the gates with her hoof and it swung open before them.

They walked on through an archway and into the castle, where unicorns were running to and fro, their hoofs clattering over the marble floor. The castle itself seemed strangely calm and peaceful against the noise within. Its walls were gleaming white, and huge windows bathed the castle in a golden light.

"Hello!" Astra called out. "Excuse me…"

But no one stopped to listen to her.

"These are the Castle Unicorns," explained Astra. "They come from all over the island to serve the King and study the spell books. But I've never seen them like this before…"

At last, Astra caught the attention of a large unicorn with a dark mane and tail, and glittering black eyes.

"That's Orion," Astra whispered to Zoe, as

he swept over to them. "He's Guardian of the Spells. He makes sure unicorns aren't misusing their magic."

"Greetings," said Orion. "I'm sure I recognize you... Ah! I know!" His eyes took in the silver stars on her coat. "You must be

Astra, Sorrel's daughter. I'm afraid this isn't a good time for your visit. There's been a theft, which is why we're all in uproar. The Grimoire has been stolen and there's no sign of the Unicorn King. We think he must have gone in search of it."

Astra gasped in horror. *"The Grimoire,"* she whispered.

"What's that?" asked Zoe.

Orion glanced at her curiously.

"This is Zoe," Astra explained. "My mother sent us here together."

"If you have Sorrel's blessing then I'm sure I can trust you," said Orion.

His words were pleasant but his expression was hard to read. There was something about his gleaming black eyes that made

Zoe feel uncomfortable.

"The Grimoire is a magical book," Orion went on. "It has all our most secret spells – both good and evil. If someone's stolen it they'll be able to wreak havoc on the island. It's usually kept in a casket in the topmost tower."

"Do you know who stole it?" asked Astra.

"The thief left no clues," said Orion, his voice abrupt. "I'm sorry I can't tell you any more. As you can see, we have much to do." He turned to go, but Astra called out after him.

"Wait!" she cried. "We came because we need the King's help too. All the trees in the forest are dying. My mother is trying to save them, but none of the spells are working."

Orion stopped in his tracks, a frown creasing his brow. "These things could all be connected," he said. "We have to track down the Unicorn King…fast. I'll gather the Castle Unicorns together. Everyone needs to hear this."

He rushed through an archway and into a cobbled courtyard. Without another word, Zoe and Astra followed him. At the centre of the courtyard stood a large, golden bell. Orion struck it three times and its peal echoed around the castle.

Zoe glanced back to watch as the unicorns came streaming through the archway. That was when she saw a feathered arrow in the castle wall, pinning down a piece of faded parchment.

"Oh, Astra," she said. "Look!"

Together, they read
the message…

I, Shadow, the Dark Leader,
have imprisoned the Unicorn
King and cast a spell across
Unicorn Island, so that all the
trees will die. When the last
tree falls at sunset, the King
will lose his power, and I shall
become your ruler.

The clock is ticking.

Soon you will
bow to me…

Chapter Four

Both Zoe and Astra stood still for a moment,
staring at the note in disbelief.

"Orion!" Astra called. He too had seen the
note. When all the unicorns had gathered
round, he read it aloud.

"Who's Shadow?" asked a young unicorn, his
eyes wide. "Have you heard of him?"

Orion nodded. "I have... He's an evil fairy

pony from Pony Island, across the sea. He tried to take over Pony Island many times. He must have stolen the Grimoire. If I'd guessed that he might come here, I would have protected our spell books."

"He says he's imprisoned the Unicorn King," said another unicorn, "but where? We've searched the whole of the castle. He could be *anywhere* on the island…"

At this, all the unicorns began talking at once, some suggesting where to look, others insisting it would be better to try to hunt down Shadow first. But then an old unicorn came forward, his long silvery beard swishing from side to side as he walked. As soon as he opened his mouth, the others fell silent, listening to him with respect.

"The Grimoire will have given Shadow enough power to imprison the King, but not to fight him or take him away," explained the old unicorn. "I have heard of Shadow, and have learned a little of how his evil mind works. In his note, Shadow tells us that he has cast a spell on our trees. It is my guess that this is where we must look for our King…imprisoned in one of our trees. He can't be far."

"Thank you, Magus," said Orion. "We will follow your advice. Let's split up and search the trees in the palace gardens."

There was a flurry of wings and the Castle Unicorns took off in all directions, until only Zoe and Astra were left.

Zoe looked at the note again. "That line about the Unicorn King losing his power when the last tree falls," she asked. "What does it mean?"

"It's part of Unicorn Law," Astra explained. "It's the King's role to protect the island. If he fails, he no longer has the right to rule. And without a king, Shadow can seize control. There would be no one powerful enough to stop him."

"But that's terrible!" cried Zoe.

"I know," said Astra. "That's why we have to find the King."

"Then why aren't we looking with the others?" asked Zoe.

"I'm trying to work something out," Astra replied. "I think it's because I can't do magic," she explained. "I like having everything clear in my head before I act." She smiled at Zoe. "Does that seem odd?"

Zoe shook her head. If Astra was a puzzle, then she felt like she'd just unlocked another part of her. Astra's quietness, her hestitation, wasn't just shyness, Zoe realized. She was always working things out, her mind one step ahead.

"If the King is trapped in a tree," Astra went on, "it can't just be any old tree. It has to be hollow, or one like a cage… I was thinking of all the trees of the forest, and the ones I have studied…"

"Go on," said Zoe, encouragingly.

Astra paused a moment, and Zoe stayed silent, sensing that she needed time to think.

"I know!" said Astra suddenly. "A weeping willow! And I've just remembered that there's one in the castle gardens, on the far side of the lake. Let's try it now."

"Brilliant!" said Zoe. She grinned at her, and Astra smiled right back. Then Astra kneeled again so that Zoe could climb on her back. They cantered out of the courtyard through the castle gardens, passing beautiful rose bowers, riotous flower beds bursting with colour and lawns dotted with statues.

"Over there!" Zoe cried suddenly, seeing the rise and fall of fountains in a crystal-clear lake. "The willow tree must be just beyond it."

"I see it," said Astra. She bent down to let Zoe slip off her back, and together they raced around the lake until they were standing before the weeping-willow tree, its arched branches falling to the ground like waves.

"On no!" cried Astra. "I can hardly bear to look!"

It was no ordinary willow tree. Shadow's curse had turned it into a great domed cage, with lethal black spikes sprouting from the branches. And, just visible behind its tangled lacework of leaves, was the Unicorn King.

Zoe and Astra rushed over to him.

"Stand back!" he called out. "The spikes are sharp. I don't want you to get hurt."

Astra stopped in her tracks and then slowly, carefully, they approached the tree.

Even within his cage, the Unicorn King looked magnificent. He was far bigger than the other unicorns Zoe had met, with a shining mane and tail. His coat was beautiful, sleek and smooth, and on his head he wore a glimmering crown.

"We saw Shadow's note," said Astra, her

words coming out in a rush. "The Castle Unicorns are out looking for you too. They'll be here soon. You must tell us what we can do to help."

"Thank you," said the King, "but first, I must hear news of the island. After he imprisoned me here, Shadow swore he was going to cast a spell on the trees. Is that why you're here, Astra? Are the trees in trouble?"

"Yes, Your Highness," Astra replied. "The trees in our forest started dying this morning. My mother thinks it's just a matter of time before the curse spreads across the island. She's tried everything she can to save them but nothing is working."

Zoe saw sorrow flood into the Unicorn King's eyes as he hung his head. Then, shaking his mane, he looked up once more.

"This is Zoe," Astra went on. "She found her way to us from the human world and wants to help. What can we do? How can we free you?"

"Welcome, Zoe," said the Unicorn King, his voice deep and solemn. "And thank you for your offer of help. Our priority now is to save the trees. Only then will I be free."

"But do you know *how* we can save the trees?" asked Astra softly.

"I have been racking my brains ever since Shadow trapped me here," the Unicorn King replied. "I think I know the way, but it is dangerous. Only a unicorn with a deep knowledge of the trees will be able to help, and we don't have much time. By sundown, Shadow's spell will be complete."

He began to pace around his cage.

"Astra," he said, "I need you to fly back to your mother and pass on this message:

beyond my castle lies the easternmost point of the island — the Ragged Cliffs that give way to the Eastern Sea. Jutting out from those cliffs is the lyra tree."

Astra nodded. "I've heard my mother speak of it," she said.

"Good," replied the Unicorn King. "Then she'll know that on it grows a single purple flower that must be picked with care. Please ask her to bring it to me. Then I can make it into a potion to save the trees."

"We'll go at once," said Astra.

"One more thing," said the King. "Give Sorrel this bag, so she can use it to carry the lyra flower. The bag will protect its powers until I can make it into a potion." As he spoke, he passed a small bag through the bars of the thorny cage.

Zoe took it from him,
and placed it
around her neck.
Its strap was
made of a thin,
shining thread, beautiful but
strong. The pouch of the bag was silky, but
Zoe could feel its surprising toughness
between her fingertips.

"Thank you, both of you," said the King.
"It was brave of you to come this far, Astra. I
always knew you were made for great
things."

"*Me?*" gasped Astra.

"Yes," said the King, gravely. "Don't doubt
your powers, Astra. Now go, and fly well."

As they turned to leave, they saw Orion and the other Castle Unicorns galloping towards them.

"He's in there," said Zoe, pointing back towards the willow tree. "But we've got to go. He's sent us on a mission."

Astra had already begun beating her wings, rising fast towards the skies. For a moment, it looked as if Orion would go after

them, but then he called out "Good luck!"
and ran to the Unicorn King.

Astra headed over the castle and Zoe could
tell she was flying as fast as she could, her tail
fanning out behind her in the wind. She
shivered as she noticed
the sun slipping
down in
the sky.

Time was already running out.

"Do you think we'll make it?" Zoe asked, as they began swooping over the valley. "We've got to fly all the way back to the forest and then your mother will have to fly to the Ragged Cliffs."

"I don't know," said Astra.

There was a moment's silence between them.

"Do you think," said Zoe, "that we should try to find the flower ourselves?"

"Well," said Astra, "as it happens that's *exactly* what I was thinking!"

She wheeled around and hovered in mid-air, as if she was unable to decide which way to go.

"There's just one small problem..." she went on. "I've heard of the lyra tree. It grows on the stormiest part of the coast. Half the day it's below tide, and when it's above tide, it's pounded by sky-high waves. Because its flower is so magical, many unicorns have tried to reach it before…but all of them have failed."

"I see," said Zoe, taking a deep breath. "But that doesn't change anything. I still think we have to get the flower ourselves. We don't have a choice. Look at the sun. It's already low in the sky."

"Are you sure?" asked Astra. "It's going to be dangerous. And I don't have any magic to protect us."

"I'm sure," Zoe replied. "Let's do it!"

Chapter Five

Astra wheeled around until they were facing the cliffs and the Eastern Sea. Zoe could feel Astra's wings, beating fast, cutting a path through the sky. Her fingers slipped through Astra's silky soft mane and she bent low so that Astra's shining coat was pressed against her cheek.

"I've never done anything like this before,"

said Astra,
as they made
their way
towards
the sea.
"Because
I can't do
magic, my mother's
always kept me close to her side, as if I need
extra protection..."

"Are you scared?" asked Zoe.

Then she looked down, and saw fierce
determination in Astra's eyes.

"No," she said. "Not being able to do
magic doesn't make me afraid. I suppose it's
just always made me feel a little alone. But I
know we can do this together."

They were silent after that as Astra flew low against the rugged coastline, battling against the strong winds that rushed over the cliff tops. From here, Zoe could see how many of the trees had already been affected by Shadow's wicked spell. Great swathes of woodland had cast their rainbow leaves to the wind and their trunks were limp and drooping.

"We must get the flower," Zoe whispered to herself. "We must save the island." And she knew that a part of her wanted to succeed for Astra too.

But as soon as they crested the cliff tops, Zoe's heart began to pound. The lyra tree stood out against the cliff face, its purple flower a single splash of colour against the shining white of the rock. The tree grew at a near-impossible angle, its roots stretched, web-like, across the cliff. Beneath it, the sea churned and frothed as if it were being whipped up by unseen hands. As Astra hovered on a gust of wind, they watched the waves. Every few minutes or so another great blanket of water rushed up against the side of the cliff, smothering the tree, before withdrawing and surging back once more.

"It's constantly being drenched," said Astra at last. "How are we ever going to reach the flower?"

"I don't know," said Zoe, "but we have to try. Let's watch and wait a little while longer."

"But there's nowhere for us to land,"

Astra pointed out. "I'll tire soon, hovering
in this wind. We can't wait long."

For the next few minutes, the two of them
tensely watched the warring waves, looking
for a pattern. They were waiting for the water
to roll back for the longest moment.

"Now!" said Zoe suddenly. "This is our
chance."

Astra arched her wings and swooped down towards the lyra tree, her long, graceful tail streaming out behind her.

As they neared the tree, Zoe stretched out her arms towards the flower and began to tug at its stem. She could hear the whirring of Astra's wings and knew how tiring this must be for her, but the flower wasn't moving.

"Keep pulling," said Astra, "and I'll keep an eye on the waves."

"It's not coming!" said Zoe. "It must be part of its magic. I can't pull it away from the tree."

"And the waves are coming back!" cried Astra. "Hold tight."

Zoe turned just in time to see a towering wave storming towards them. For a moment,

she thought they weren't going to make it,
but on spray-drenched wings Astra brought
them safely out of reach.

"Did you get the flower?" asked Astra.

"No!" said Zoe, feeling close to tears. "I
think there's a special secret to it. Your mother
must know it, but there's no time to get to her
now, and I know you're running out of
strength. Do you have any idea what the
secret might be?"

Zoe could see the desperation on Astra's
face. "Let me think a moment…the lyra
flower. My mother has taught me so much of
what she knows, she's sure to have taught me
this. Oh! If only I could remember!"

In panic, she gazed for a moment at the
sun, then suddenly her eyes flashed with

inspiration. "Of course!" she cried. "You have to turn it from east to west and back again, just like the path of the sun. Can you try that now?"

"Okay," said Zoe. "I really hope it works."

Once again, they watched the waves, and as soon as they rolled back Astra dived down

to the tree. This time Zoe turned the flower as Astra had suggested, trying to ignore her freezing hands and numbed fingers.

"It's coming! I can feel it loosening," she cried. Zoe gave it a final turn. "I've got it!" she shouted triumphantly, placing it in her bag.

Just then a huge wave began to roll in.

Astra began to beat her wings but then Zoe cried out, "Stop! The bag – it's caught on the branches."

"You'll have to leave it," said Astra. "That wave is coming in fast."

"But then the bag will be swept away. We'll lose the flower. We will have failed…"

Zoe knew that Astra didn't have the strength to keep going. There was only one thing for it.

"Fly to safety," she cried.

As soon as the words were out of her mouth, she leaped from Astra's back. With one hand she clung to the tree, and with the other, she held tightly on to the bag. She had never felt so scared or so certain of anything in her life. She couldn't bear to lose that flower.

She watched Astra swoop up and away, but the next moment the little winged unicorn was blotted from view by the towering waves.

Chapter Six

Zoe clung to the tree, eyes tight shut, as the waves pounded against her. The water was freezing cold and she had to gasp for air each time the waves withdrew.

But she knew she couldn't let go…she couldn't risk losing the bag, or being swept out to sea. The sea water drenched through her clothes, plastering her hair to her face,

and trying, with
its surging force, to
prise her away from
the branches. Then, just
as she thought she couldn't hold
on any longer, Astra was beside her.

Zoe untangled the bag from the
branches and reached for Astra's neck.
Then, with one final exhausted effort,
she slid from the tree onto Astra's back.

"You're safe now," Astra whispered.
"We made it!"

They soared over the cliff tops, and it

was only when the sea was safely behind them that Astra spoke again. "I was so worried, Zoe. I thought you were going to be swept away by the sea. I can't believe how brave you were."

"No braver than you," said Zoe. "I don't know how you kept going for so long. Just shows you don't need magic to make things happen." She grinned.

"We're a great team," laughed Astra. After that, she flew hard and fast to the castle, as if her energy had been renewed by the thought of the healing flower.

As soon as they reached the Unicorn King, Zoe tumbled from Astra's back and handed him the precious bag through the thorns.

"What's this?" he asked.

In all the excitement, Zoe had forgotten they had disobeyed his instructions.

"We…we found the flower," said Astra. "I know you asked us to fetch my mother, but we were worried that there wouldn't be enough time. So we went ourselves. But we did it — look inside the bag! The lyra flower is there."

The Unicorn King frowned. "I would never have asked you to put yourselves in danger like that," he said.

He looked from Zoe to Astra, taking in Zoe's dripping clothes and wet hair and Astra's heaving flanks.

"You must never risk your lives like that again. But for now, all I can say is thank you."

Then, for the first time, Zoe saw him smile.

"Now, I must set to work," he said.

Zoe and Astra watched in fascination as the Unicorn King placed the purple flower at his feet. He began pounding it with his hoofs, chanting a spell as he went. Soon the flower began to burn with a bright flame. A sweet smell rose from the

willow tree in a plume of purple smoke. The Unicorn King began to chant another spell, and Zoe could just catch the words:

Lyra flower, sweet and pure
Burn bright, burn clear,
Create a potion that will cure
Our trees, so dear.

When the flames died down, a gentle wind whipped up the petals of the flower. Zoe watched as they were transformed into a glittering purple powder that streamed back into the bag.

"Here," said the Unicorn King, passing the bag back through the thorns. "This may seem like a small amount but it's incredibly powerful. A tiny sprinkle over a woodland will restore the trees to health. There should be enough there, I hope, to cure all the trees on the island. Take it, and spread its magic."

Zoe took the bag and held it reverently in her hands.

"But what about *you*?" she asked.

"When the last tree is saved, I will be freed from my prison," said the Unicorn King. "Now go!"

"Thank you," said Zoe, jumping onto Astra's back.

"Goodbye!" Astra called, as they rose into the sky. "I can't bear leaving him like this," she said to Zoe, her voice wavering, "trapped in that evil prison."

"Don't worry," said Zoe. "Together we're going to free him. I know it. Where should we go first?"

"Let's start with the trees in the palace gardens," said Astra. "Then we'll have to circle round the valley, and hope the wind carries more of the powder to reach all the trees in time."

As she spoke, Astra swooped low over a wooded glade in the castle gardens, where Orion and the other Castle Unicorns were trying to support the fading trees.

"Now!" cried Astra, and Zoe dipped into the bag and sprinkled the trees with a tiny pinch of the magical powder.

The trees rose
up and up,
their
trunks
becoming
straight, their branches
once again reaching for the sky.
Finally new, rainbow-coloured, glittering
leaves sprouted from the tips of the branches,
fluttering on the breeze.

The Castle Unicorns watched, amazed, then looked up at Astra and Zoe and cheered.

"Isn't it incredible!" said Zoe.

"But there's no time to stop," said Astra, scything through the air once more. "We'll cure the trees along the coast next."

Far and wide they flew over Unicorn Island, Zoe sprinkling the magical powder and Astra flying on, urgently, conscious of the sinking sun.

As last they came to the wooded glade where their journey had begun. There, Sorrel was anxiously waiting from them. She galloped over as soon as they landed.

"Astra!" she called. "I heard the news from the birds that Shadow imprisoned the Unicorn King and cursed the trees. I've been so worried about you both. What's taken you so long?"

"Here," said Zoe, showing her the bag. "We have the cure for the trees. These are the last in need of the healing powder."

Sorrel bent her neck and sniffed the bag. "Of course!" she cried. "The lyra flower! But who was able to get it?"

"We did," said Astra, half-proudly, half-afraid of her mother's reaction.

"No!" gasped Sorrel, her face turning ghostly white with fear. "You've been in so much danger." She nuzzled her daughter close to her side.

"I know it was a risk," said Astra, "but we're safe now. And it's all because you taught me so well."

"Here," said Zoe, passing

Sorrel the bag of glittering purple

powder. "This is for you."

"Thank you," said Sorrel, smiling.

She took the bag between her teeth and then fluttered her wings, launching herself into the air. Zoe and Astra watched as she swooped over the glade, the lyra powder streaming behind her, sparkling in the evening sun.

A moment later, the glade had sprung back to life. The silver bark once again shone with a magical light and the woodland animals began to creep out from their hiding places. Deer pranced between the slender, shining trunks, squirrels leaped between the branches

and rabbits peered out shyly from the bushes. And then Zoe heard it…the sound of the birds returning. The air was filled with their song and the unicorns joined in the celebration, taking to the air, swooping and diving as they soared over the treetops.

A moment later, the sky was lit with pink streaks, cast by the setting sun.

"We did it!" cried Zoe, running over to Astra and flinging her arms around her neck. "We saved the trees before sunset. Does that mean Shadow has been beaten?"

"It does," said a deep and majestic voice.

Zoe looked up and gasped. There was the Unicorn King, free at last.

Chapter Seven

Standing proudly in the centre of the glade, the Unicorn King looked even more magnificent now he was out of his cage. His coat shone and the crown on his head gleamed with a magical power of its own. Zoe found herself awed just to be in his presence and, for a moment, she found she was lost for words.

"How did you get here so quickly?" she asked at last.

The King laughed. "My powers have been restored to me," he said, "and one of them is great speed. I wanted to come here first of all, to thank you both for saving the island."

He caught Sorrel's eye and smiled ruefully. "I never meant for them to go looking for the lyra flower. I had asked them to fetch *you*."

Sorrel shook her head at them. "I will scold them later," she said. "I can't be angry now. I am too overjoyed that our trees, and our King, have been restored to us."

"Well then," said the Unicorn King, "I think it's time for a celebration."

He bowed his head. There was a flash of silver light, and a crackle of golden sparkles

shot out from the King's horn.
When Zoe looked down, the
ground at her feet was piled high

with plates of food — cakes

and fruit and succulent
sweets, baskets
brimming with
nuts and berries and jugs of
delicious-smelling juice.

Then the Unicorn King
threw back his head and whinnied, long and
loud. At the sound, all the Forest Unicorns
gathered around him, cheering
to see him safe again.

"Let the feast begin!" announced the
Unicorn King.

The glade, glowing in the light of the

setting sun, was more magical than ever. While the Forest Unicorns danced and sang, Astra and Zoe sat quietly together, exhausted after all their adventures.

"This is the most delicious food I've ever tasted," said Zoe. "The cake is so sweet it tastes like…"

"…honeydew?" asked Astra. "That's what it's made from. And these little ones are apple blossom and nectar."

"Maybe I've got room for one more, then," grinned Zoe. "After all, it's not often that I get to eat enchanted food." She paused, remembering something but unsure whether she should bring it up. "What do you think the Unicorn King meant," she asked at last, "about you not doubting your powers?

Maybe he thinks you'll be able to do magic one day."

"I don't know," Astra replied. "I was wondering that, too." She smiled, and Zoe noticed how the dappled light from the trees lit up the stars on her coat, so that they sparkled like the night sky. "But for now," said Astra, tossing her mane, "I'm going to stop worrying about not being able to do magic. After all, we did pretty well today without it."

"Well," said Zoe. "*I* think there's something *extra* magical about you, whatever happens. Oh," she sighed. "I wish I could stay here for ever."

But as the sunset faded and night drew in, Sorrel and the Unicorn King came over to join them.

"It is time for you to return to your own world," he said. "I know from our spell books that time passes faster here than it does in your world, so if you return now, it will still be night in your world, and you can sleep.

But first," the Unicorn King continued, "I want to give you this, as a way of saying thank you for all you did today."

He pulled a tiny flask from a bag around his neck. "This is Magic Dust," he explained. "It means you can return to Unicorn Island whenever you want. A tiny pinch will shrink you down to fairy size so you can travel through the tunnel in the Great Oak. And hidden within the bag, is a spell. Chant the words to light the way to Unicorn Island. Please, visit us again."

"I will," Zoe promised.

"We may need your help again sooner than you think," the King added solemnly. "Shadow still has the Grimoire and he's not one to give up easily. We are not safe yet."

"I'll always do what I can to help Unicorn Island," said Zoe.

"Yes," said the King. "I believe you will. I have a feeling you were sent to us in this time of trouble."

He smiled once more, then he and Sorrel rose up on their majestic wings, and were lost among the inky folds of the night sky.

"Goodbye!" Zoe called.

"Will you really come back?" said Astra, moving closer to Zoe.

"Of course I will," said Zoe, grinning. "Just try to stop me!"

She followed Astra
to the entrance to
the Great Oak
and wrapped her
arms around her silky
neck one last time.
"Goodbye, for now," she
said, drawing herself away.

Astra whinnied gently, her black eyes
shining. Zoe gave one last wave and ran into
the tunnel. This time, there was a path of light,
guiding her back the way she'd come.

When she reached the entrance to her own
world, she stepped out into Great-Aunt May's
garden. For a moment she worried she would
always be fairy-sized, as she gazed up at the
towering grasses. Then a tingling feeling began

in her toes and fingertips. It was followed by a loud whooshing noise, and then a shower of sparkles appeared before her eyes. When she next looked down, she realized she was her old height again.

"Magic," murmured Zoe. Then, unable to resist, she crouched down and peered back between the roots of the oak tree.

Did I dream it? Zoe wondered for a moment.

But then her eyes caught sight of the little flask in the palm of her hand, filled with sparkling powder. "It really did happen," she whispered. "I can't wait to tell Holly all about it. And I can't wait to go back for more magical adventures…"

Enter the world of the

Fairy Unicorns

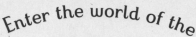

and collect every
enchanting tale

Magic Forest   ISBN: 9781474926898

Zoe is staying with her great-aunt when she discovers
a magical world full of fairy unicorns – hidden at the
bottom of the garden. But Zoe soon finds out that
Unicorn Island is in terrible danger.

Cloud Castle   ISBN: 9781474926904

Zoe and her friend Astra can't wait for the
Midsummer Festival. But Unicorn Island is
growing hotter and hotter… Has Shadow,
the evil fairy pony, stolen the clouds?

Coming soon...

Wind Charm ISBN: 9781474926911

When Zoe visits Unicorn Island she mistakenly opens the
Box of Winds, unleashing a terrible storm over the island.
Can Zoe and her best friend, Astra, the fairy unicorn,
stop the winds before it's too late?

Enchanted River ISBN: 9781474926928

When Zoe discovers the island is flooding, she knows
she has to stop the waters – and fast. Is there any way
for Zoe and her best friend Astra, the fairy unicorn,
to save the island from disaster?

Frost Fair ISBN: 9781474926935

Winter's arrived on Unicorn Island, and Zoe can't
wait to visit the Frost Fair with her best friend Astra.
But when cursed snowflakes begin falling, the unicorns
are turned to ice. Who could be behind this evil plan –
and can Zoe and Astra stop them?

Star Spell ISBN: 9781474926942

The time has come to defeat Shadow, the evil fairy pony,
once and for all, and Zoe returns to Unicorn
Island to help. But her best friend, Astra, is in
terrible danger, and only Zoe can save her...

If you've loved Fairy Unicorns, why
not enter the world of the

Fairy Ponies

Midnight Escape   ISBN: 9781409506287

Holly is staying with her Great-Aunt May when she
discovers a tiny pony with shimmering wings. At first
she thinks she must be dreaming…until two fairy
ponies visit her with an urgent mission.

Magic Necklace   ISBN: 9781409506294

Holly and her friend Puck are visiting the Pony Queen
when a magical necklace is stolen from the palace.
Can Puck and Holly help track it down before
the thief uses its magic?

Rainbow Races   ISBN: 9781409506300

Holly can't wait to watch her friend Puck compete in the
Rainbow Races. But when an enchanted storm is
unleashed over Pony Island, ruining the races, the home
of the fairy ponies is threatened with darkness for ever...

Pony Princess   ISBN: 9781409506379

When the Fairy Pony Princess comes to visit, Puck and
Holly are given the all-important job of looking after her.
But then their royal guest goes missing. Can Puck
and Holly find her again?

Unicorn Prince   ISBN: 9781409506362

Holly and Puck uncover a wicked plot to take
over Pony Island. To save the day, they must
venture into the Enchanted Wood, home of the
mysterious unicorns...

Enchanted Mirror   ISBN: 9781409506386

Pony Island is in danger. The ponies are losing their
magic and the Pony Queen's powers are under threat.
Can Holly and Puck uncover the mystery of the
missing magic, before it's too late?

Edited by Becky Walker

Designed by Brenda Cole

Reading consultant: Alison Kelly

First published in 2017 by Usborne Publishing Ltd.,
Usborne House, 83-85 Saffron Hill, London EC1N 8RT, England.
www.usborne.com

Copyright © Usborne Publishing, 2017

Illustrations copyright © Usborne Publishing, 2017

Front cover and inside illustrations by Nuno Vieira Alexandre

The name Usborne and the devices ♀ 🌐 are Trade Marks of
Usborne Publishing Ltd.

A CIP catalogue record for this book is available from the British Library.